Art by Keiron Ward for Artful Doodlers Ltd.

Book Design by Yaffa Jaskoll

Published by Scholastic Australia in 2024.

Scholastic Australia Pty Limited
PO Box 579 Gosford NSW 2250
ABN 11 000 614 577
www.scholastic.com.au

Part of the Scholastic Group
Sydney • Auckland • New York • Toronto • London
Mexico City • New Delhi • Hong Kong • Buenos Aires • Puerto Rico

ISBN 978-1-76152-742-5

Printed in China.

Scholastic Australia's policy, in association with its printers, is to use papers that are renewable and made efficiently from wood grown in responsibly managed forests, so as to minimise its environmental footprint.

FEELINGS ARE BETTER WITH

By Micol Ostow

SCHOLASTIC
SYDNEY AUCKLAND NEW YORK TORONTO LONDON MEXICO CITY
NEW DELHI HONG KONG BUENOS AIRES PUERTO RICO

FEELINGS are better with friends.

Whatever you're doing, no matter your mood,
your friends are always there for you!

Some mornings, you start your day
HAPPY enough to sing out loud.

Your musical friends—like
Phoebe—can help with that!

Cleaning and organising her apartment makes Monica feel **HAPPY.**

She loves baking treats too. And that makes everyone **HAPPY!**

Being a good friend means understanding that different things bring different people **JOY.**

For Rachel, sometimes that's a day shopping with friends.

A day at the museum makes Ross **EXCITED**—
especially if dinosaurs are involved!

A delicious sandwich always makes Joey feel **GREAT** . . .

And so does hanging with his BFF, Chandler.

Chandler **LOVES** hanging out with Joey too. They tell jokes, watch TV, play games . . .

Sometimes, they even invent new games of their own.

Feelings can be complicated.
They can change from moment to moment
or day to day.

Ross was **SAD** when his sandwich disappeared. But when he found out someone ate it, he went from **SAD** to **MAD**!

Ross even had a nickname for himself
for when he got **ANGRY:**

Ross isn't the only one who lets his emotions get the better of him.

Monica *really* likes to feel like a **WINNER.** Even if that means winning the 'Best Worst Massages' award!

A friendly game of Thanksgiving football can bring out the worst emotions in the very best of pals.

Especially when the Geller Cup is at stake!

It's normal to feel competitive sometimes.

But when friends take it too far, everyone's **UPSET.**

That's okay though.
Because a good friend knows to say sorry when they've made someone **SAD** or **MAD.**

And a friend knows how to forgive too.

Life would get pretty **LONELY** without your friends by your side.

And when you're **SCARED**,
your friends have your back.

When Ross's pants shrunk, he was **AFRAID**
he'd never be able to pull them up!
But Joey was there to help.

Friends are always there when things
get a little too **SCARY**.

Everyone feels **NERVOUS** trying something new for the first time.

When Monica started her new chef job,
she **WORRIED** that no-one would like her.

But Joey was by her side to
make her feel better.

We all feel **JEALOUS** sometimes too. Like when Rachel found out Monica went shopping without her.

I WAS THINKING OF YOU THE WHOLE TIME!

The important thing is to be there for our friends in whatever they do.

Like when the gang travelled a long way to see Joey star in a movie, only to find out it was cancelled!

He was **EMBARRASSED.**
But his friends were proud of him anyway.

Our feelings can be surprising, just like life!
But our friends are always there with
a special treat. Because . . .

THAT'S WHAT FRIENDS ARE FOR!